THIS DIARY BELONGS TO:

Vicky P

PRIVATE & CONFIDENTIAL

If found, please return to ME for REWARD!

(NO SNOOPING ALLOWED!!! ☹)

ALSO BY

Rachel Renée Russell

Dork Diaries:

Tales from a Not-So-Fabulous Life

Dork Diaries 2:

Tales from a Not-So-Popular Party Girl

Dork Diaries 3:

Tales from a Not-So-Talented Pop Star

Dork Diaries 3½:

How to Dork Your Diary

Dork Diaries 4:

Tales from a Not-So-Graceful Ice Princess

Dork Diaries 5:

Tales from a Not-So-Smart Miss Know-It-All

Dork Diaries 6:

Tales from a Not-So-Happy Heartbreaker

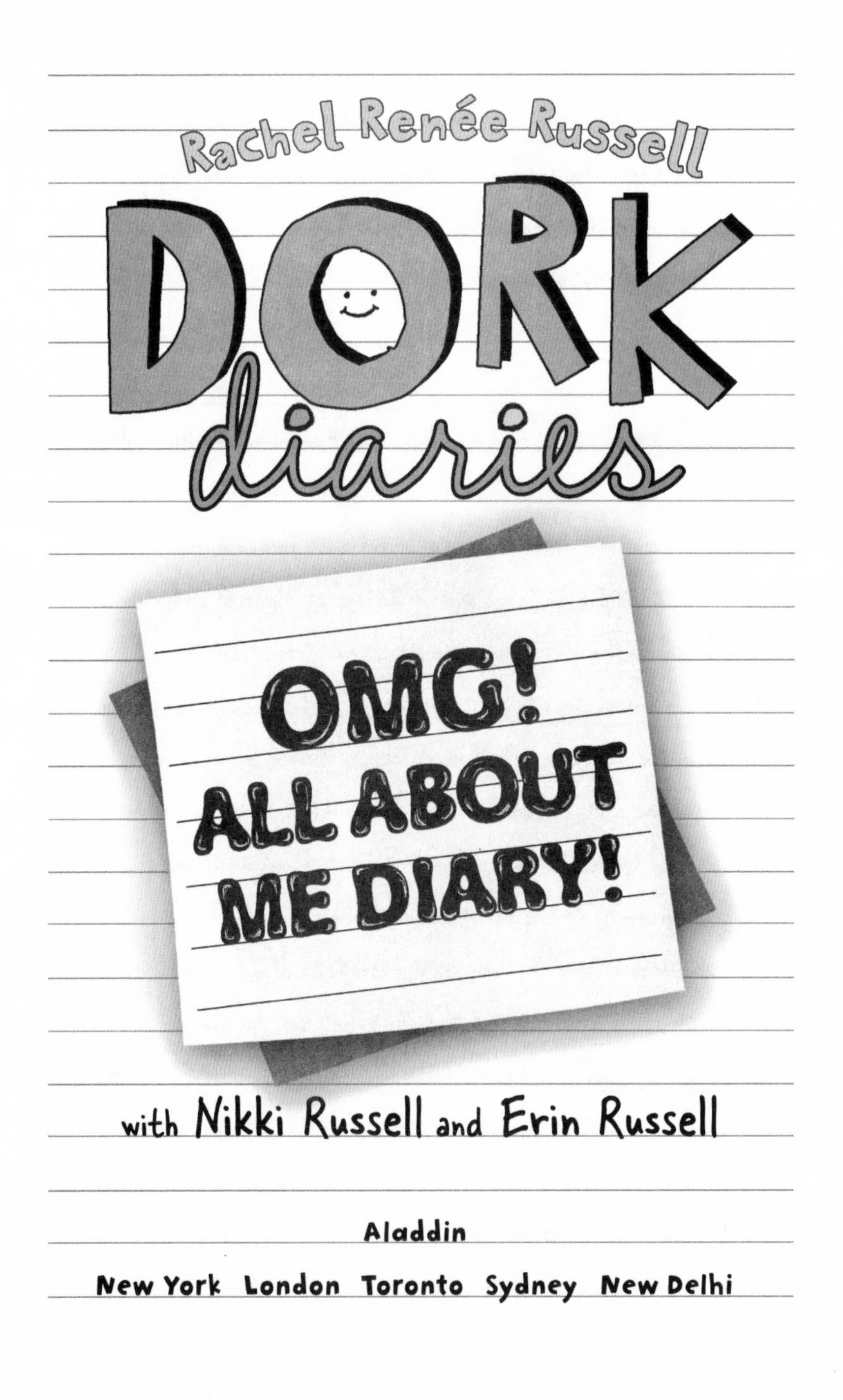
Rachel Renée Russell
DORK diaries
OMG! ALL ABOUT ME DIARY!
with Nikki Russell and Erin Russell
Aladdin
New York London Toronto Sydney New Delhi

This book is a work of fiction. Any references to historical events, real people, or real places are used fictitiously. Other names, characters, places, and events are products of the author's imagination, and any resemblance to actual events or places or persons, living or dead, is entirely coincidental.

ALADDIN * An imprint of Simon & Schuster Children's Publishing Division * 1230 Avenue of the Americas, New York, NY 10020 * First Aladdin hardcover edition October 2013 * * For information about special discounts for bulk purchases, please contact Simon & Schuster Special Sales at 1-866-506-1949 or business@simonandschuster.com. * The Simon & Schuster Speakers Bureau can bring authors to your live event. For more information or to book an event contact the Simon & Schuster Speakers Bureau at 1-866-248-3049 or visit our website at www.simonspeakers.com. * Series design by Lisa Vega * Book design by Jeanine Henderson * The text of this book was set in Skippy Sharp. * Manufactured in the United States of America 0813 FFG * 10 9 8 7 6 5 4 3 2 1 * Library of Congress Cataloging-in-Publication Data * Russell, Rachel Renée, author, illustrator. * Dork diaries : OMG! All about me diary! / by Rachel Renée Russell. * p. cm. * 1. Diaries—Authorship—Juvenile literature. 2. Autobiography—Authorship—Juvenile literature. I. Title. II. Title: All about me diary! * PN4390.R866 2013 * 808.06'692—dc23 * 2013020049 * ISBN 978-1-4424-8771-0 * ISBN 978-1-4424-8772-7 (eBook)

☺ Dedicated to YOU, my BFF ☺!

Love, Nikki Maxwell

INTRODUCTION

Fellow Dorks, grab your pens!

If you're a diary fanatic like ME, you are SO going to love your *OMG! All About Me Diary!* This book is filled with 365 questions, plus a bonus question (written by yours truly) that'll have you thinking, laughing, and learning surprising new things about yourself.

You'll have fun writing about the JUICIEST gossip, the funniest stories, and your most embarrassing moments! I'll also ask you to share your dreams, wishes, and secret thoughts.

You can write in your diary every single day for TWO whole years! And when you read these memories, you'll be amazed at how much you've changed or stayed the same.

I came up with all these questions myself. And to keep things interesting, I've actually spilled my guts and answered a few of them. But, hey, I'm not worried! I know I can totally trust you with my secrets ☺!

You can start your diary on January 1 or today's date. If you happen to miss a day, don't sweat it! You can always go back and fill it in later.

Have fun, and happy writing! And always remember to let your inner Dork shine through.

Your dorkalicious friend,

Nikki Maxwell

☺

JANUARY

JANUARY 1: Why should YOU be crowned PRINCESS of the DORKS?

YEAR 1: because i'm fabulous.

YEAR 2:

JANUARY 2: What is your New Year's resolution? Why is this important to you? What can you do TODAY to help you achieve it?

YEAR 1: To eat less, why? so i can't get fat, today? eat healthier (not gonna happen)

YEAR 2:

JANUARY 3: "Mirror, mirror, on the wall . . . !" If you could ask your MAGIC looking glass anything and get the honest truth, WHAT would you ask it?

YEAR 1: ~~Who's~~ Why is Tiffany (girl i hate) still alive?

YEAR 2:

JANUARY 4: You have a tall, steaming mug of hot chocolate! Extra whipped cream or extra marshmallows?

YEAR 1: Both! :)

YEAR 2:

JANUARY 5: What message would you like to find in a fortune cookie? Why?

YEAR 1: You would meet your fave youtuber and celeb♡ Why? because i love them ♡

YEAR 2:

JANUARY 6: Which three songs could you listen to one hundred times and never get tired of hearing them? What NEW song do you need to add to your playlist?

YEAR 1:
- Sweet Dreams By Kalin & Myles [KAM]
- Pompeii by Bastile
- Play it again by Becky G.

Add: Play it again (Becky G) & more :)

YEAR 2:

JANUARY 7: Look in the mirror and finish this sentence: My ______________ is/are SUPERCUTE!

YEAR 1: ~~Skater skirt~~ top

YEAR 2:

JANUARY 8: If you could be any other person in the world for ONE WEEK, who would it be and why?

YEAR 1: Bethany Mota because she's perf.

YEAR 2:

JANUARY 9: Someone just left a HUGE package on your doorstep with YOUR name on it! What do you hope is inside?

NIKKI'S ANSWER: ART SUPPLIES ☺!
SQUEEE!!

YEAR 1: tickets (concert tickets & meet & greet tickets)

YEAR 2:

JANUARY 10: Have you ever been SO embarrassed you wanted to dig a deep hole, crawl into it, and DIE?! Details, please!

YEAR 1: No. oops.

YEAR 2:

JANUARY 11: You just got stuck babysitting Brianna! YIKES! What will you do to entertain her?

YEAR 1: give her food and let her watch TV. :)

YEAR 2:

JANUARY 12: Do you feel SWEET, SOUR, or SPICY?

NIKKI'S ANSWER: I feel sour. Mostly because I need a shower. Really BAD!

YEAR 1: Sweet ♡

YEAR 2:

JANUARY 13: Chloe and Zoey are my BFFs! Who are YOURS?

YEAR 1: Brooke (Besty) :)
Jacqueline (sister / bff)
Cassey (Besty-half)

YEAR 2:

JANUARY 14: What TV show are you totally obsessed with right now, and what show do you hate? Why?

YEAR 1: TV show? love: full house, etc.
hate: idk.

YEAR 2:

JANUARY 15: I know you've been taking a sneak peek at my Dork Diaries! Hey, who can resist reading them?! Which one is your most favorite and why?

YEAR 1: haven't read any. this is first book.

YEAR 2:

JANUARY 16: What's the latest dance that you know? How did you learn to do it?

BRIANNA AND ME, DOING THE HARLEM SHAKE!

YEAR 1: i know Harlem Shake, but i dont do it. LOL >.<

YEAR 2:

JANUARY 17: What's the FIERCEST outfit in your closet? Why do you love it?

YEAR 1: My Blue lace dress ♡♡ bcs it's so beautiful!

YEAR 2:

JANUARY 18: What outfit in your closet is so HIDEOUS you'd love to burn it? Why do you hate it?

NIKKI'S ANSWER: The roach costume Dad made me wear to hand out free bug inspection coupons. When I see it, I relive the trauma all over again!

YEAR 1: none

YEAR 2:

JANUARY 19: List the foods that make you want to GAG!!

YEAR 1: None.

YEAR 2:

JANUARY 20: List the foods that you LOVE, LOVE, LOVE!

YEAR 1: All. Besides salad :)

YEAR 2:

JANUARY 21: Dr. Martin Luther King Jr. had a dream that one day ALL people would be treated equally, regardless of the color of their skin. What dream do YOU have that would make the world a better place?

YEAR 1: 1. Respect others
2. Respect yourself
3. Respect Earth

YEAR 2:

JANUARY 22: You just had a really BAD day ☹! What do you do to CHILLAX?

ME, FEELING BETTER AFTER VENTING IN MY DIARY!

YEAR 1: listen to music / talk to my besty bout it.

YEAR 2:

JANUARY 23: Who's the KOOKIEST person in your family?

NIKKI'S ANSWER: Everyone in my family is a little nuts! But it would have to be a tie between Brianna and my grandma for the kookiest.

YEAR 1: Lily (cousin)

YEAR 2:

JANUARY 24: You're throwing the ultimate birthday party! What twelve people are on your fantasy guest list?

YEAR 1: Brooke, Jacqueline, Cassey, Kathy, Miah, Kianna, Janne, Lily, prob that's all

YEAR 2:

JANUARY 25: If YOU were a lip gloss flavor, what would you be and why? Give yourself a flavalicious name!

YEAR 1: Strawberry? maybe. &
Name: Strawberrilicious

YEAR 2:

JANUARY 26: School is canceled because of SNOW! Woo-hoo! How will you spend most of your day?

A) Snuggled in bed, catching up on sleep

B) Lounging in your pj's, reading your fave book

C) Playing outside in the snow with your BFFs

YEAR 1: none. instead Besty come to my house & use electronics :)

YEAR 2:

JANUARY 27: You have a big test tomorrow! Out of Chloe, Zoey, Brandon, and me (Nikki!), who would you choose as your STUDY BUDDY and why?

YEAR 1: IDK. Prob You.

YEAR 2:

JANUARY 28: What was the last thing that made you so ANGRY you wanted to SCREAM?

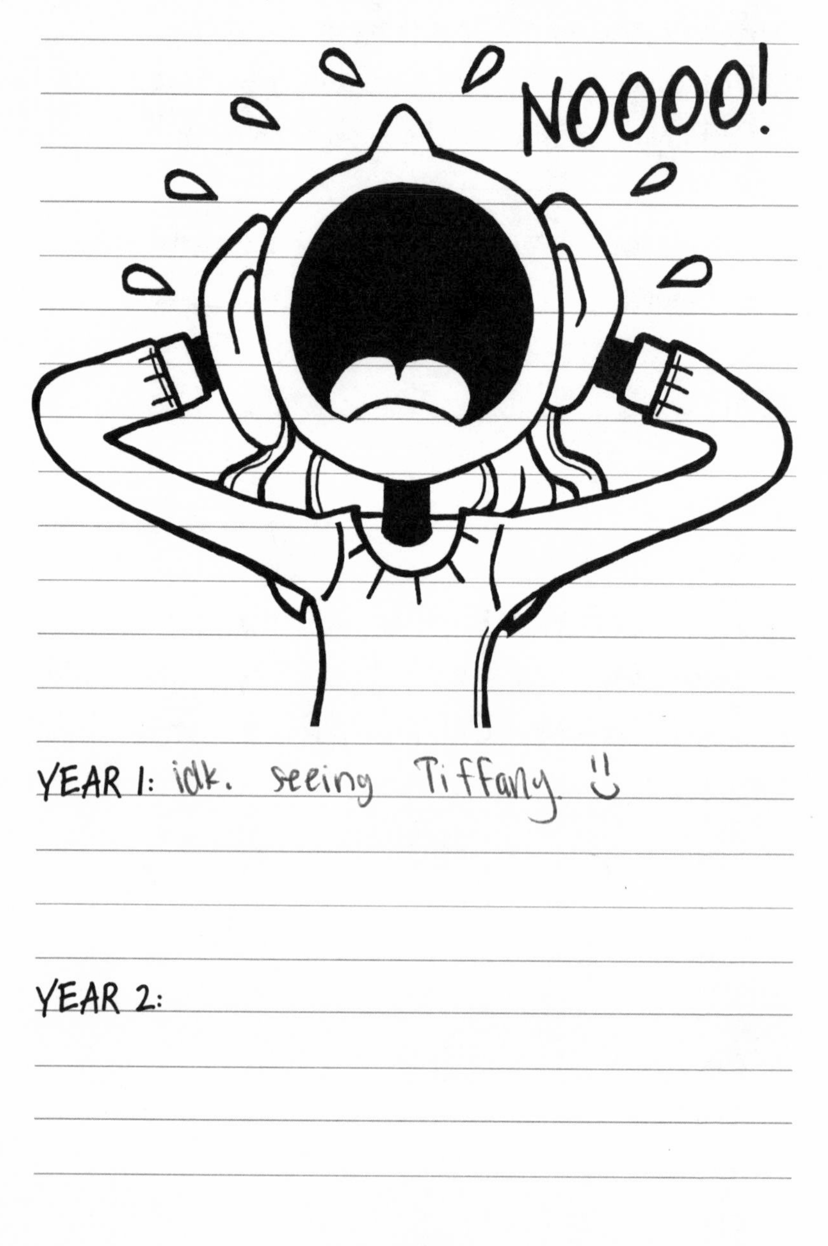

YEAR 1: idk. seeing Tiffany. ☺

YEAR 2:

JANUARY 29: What's the latest juicy GOSSIP?!

YEAR 1: iDK.

YEAR 2:

JANUARY 30: If you could hang out with a cartoon character in real life, who would it be and why?

NIKKI'S ANSWER: I'd like to hang out with SpongeBob SquarePants because he seems fun, friendly, and DORKY!

YEAR 1: Blue Clues . . . i know crazy, but he's cute!!!

YEAR 2:

JANUARY 31: If I were your fairy godmother and could grant you ONE WISH, what would you ask for?

YEAR 1: more wishes !!

YEAR 2:

FEBRUARY

FEBRUARY 1: Who are you crushing on? Why?

YEAR 1: nobody. jk. Nash grier bcs he's a funny viner.

YEAR 2:

FEBRUARY 2: In gym class, are you a scared-of-balls person, average, or a star athlete? Why do you think so?

YEAR 1: Average? bcs im not a perfect athlete, but i'm not really afraid of balls.

YEAR 2:

FEBRUARY 3: If you were principal of your school for a day, what would you do to make it more fun and exciting?

YEAR 1: Party! ? ?

YEAR 2:

FEBRUARY 4: You got trapped in the mall overnight with your BFFs ☺! Make a list of the things you would do.

YEAR 1: Get everything that's Cute!!

YEAR 2:

FEBRUARY 5: Complete this sentence: "I would absolutely DIE if my friends found out my DEEP, DARK SECRET that ____________."

YEAR 1: i have a pillow that i still sleep with.

YEAR 2:

FEBRUARY 6: Have you ever done something CRAZY to try to impress your CRUSH?

NIKKI'S ANSWER: Yes. I pretended I could ice-skate!!

YEAR 1: No.

YEAR 2:

FEBRUARY 7: Create a recipe for the crush of your dreams! (Like, 2 cups of kindness, 3 teaspoons of cuteness, etc.)

YEAR 1: 500 tsps of hotness, 3 cups Of kindness, 3 cups of trustness

YEAR 2:

FEBRUARY 8: At this moment, who do you feel the most like: ME, Chloe, Zoey, or MacKenzie? Why?

YEAR 1: you? idk why.

YEAR 2:

FEBRUARY 9: Whenever you get SUPERhappy and excited, what do you say that's probably kind of silly?

NIKKI'S ANSWER: I smile really big, close my eyes really tight, and squeal, "SQUEEEEEE!" ☺!

YEAR 1: i sqveal.

YEAR 2:

FEBRUARY 10: WHO would you LOVE to get a Valentine's Day gift from?

YEAR 1: My fave youtubers/celebs !!

YEAR 2:

FEBRUARY 11: I need your advice! What do you think I should do to show Brandon that I like him? Or should I just keep it a big secret so I don't ruin our friendship?! HELP!!

YEAR 1: give him a note :) & say "promise me no matter what we'll always be friends :)"

YEAR 2:

FEBRUARY 12: WHO or WHAT gives you a severe case of RCS (Roller-Coaster Syndrome), also known as butterflies? WHEEEE!! ☺!

YEAR 1: IDK.

YEAR 2:

FEBRUARY 13: Tomorrow is Valentine's Day! Make a list of family and friends you'd like to give a card to.

YEAR 1: Mom, Dad, Bro, everyone in class ♡ ♡ ♡ ♡

YEAR 2:

FEBRUARY 14: HAPPY VALENTINE'S DAY!

If you could design your very own CANDY HEARTS, what would they SAY? List five of them below.

YEAR 1: You're fab like Beth ♡
or ilysm (i love you so much)

YEAR 2:

FEBRUARY 15: Your school is putting on a play! Would you rather be the star of the show, the director, or the costume designer? Why?

YEAR 1: costume designer bcs ~~me~~ i get to design

YEAR 2:

FEBRUARY 16: If your life were a classic fairy tale, which one would it be and why?

YEAR 1: idk?

YEAR 2:

FEBRUARY 17: Every February we celebrate Presidents Day. Who would you rather be, the president of the United States or the First Lady? Why?

YEAR 1: president! Holla, idk why :)

YEAR 2:

FEBRUARY 18: If you won a game show, what would you want your grand prize to be?

YEAR 1: Bethany Mota ♡ YAS!

YEAR 2:

FEBRUARY 19: "My friends always tell me I'm a really good ________________!"

NIKKI'S ANSWER: I'm sure you can probably guess that everyone tells me I'm a really good ARTIST!!

YEAR 1: at being funny/nice

YEAR 2:

FEBRUARY 20: If you were an animal, which one would you be and why?

YEAR 1: giraffe bcs no harm done to them!

YEAR 2:

FEBRUARY 21: Please don't BUG OUT! But what is your most favorite insect and why? What is your least favorite insect and why?

YEAR 1: Butterfly bcs harmless
Hate: all insects bcs im
SCARed.

YEAR 2:

FEBRUARY 22: Have you ever told someone a personal secret and then THEY told someone else? What was the secret and WHO told it?

YEAR 1: NO.

YEAR 2:

FEBRUARY 23: Have you ever been told a secret that you were DYING to tell someone else? What was it? Did you keep the secret or SPILL IT?

YEAR 1: Yea. "My Bffs crush" kept it

YEAR 2:

FEBRUARY 24: What DESSERT do you LOVE so much that you would eat it for breakfast, lunch, AND dinner if you could?

YEAR 1: ice cream YAS!

YEAR 2:

FEBRUARY 25: What are you DYING to say to MacKenzie Hollister? Write it below.

YEAR 1: Uh. "Who's Maskenzie Hollister"

YEAR 2:

FEBRUARY 26: What are you DYING to say to me, Nikki Maxwell? Write it below.

YEAR 1: Who? is? she?

YEAR 2:

FEBRUARY 27: Which famous TV family is the most like yours? How are you similar?

YEAR 1: uh full house i guess, idk.

YEAR 2:

FEBRUARY 28: Pretend that your CRUSH finally asks you to hang out. What happens on your dream date?

YEAR 1: go to movies, get ice cream, and others!:)

YEAR 2:

FEBRUARY 29: Leap year only comes once every four years. What event do you wish would happen only once every four years?

NIKKI'S ANSWER: I really HATE cleaning up my bedroom! It would be REALLY nice to clean it only once every four years ☺!

LEAP YEAR: not go to school!, jk.
I wish, but iDk.

MARCH

MARCH 1: What was the last SUPERfunny thing that had you ROTFL (rolling on the floor laughing)?

YEAR 1:

YEAR 2:

MARCH 2: If you could give yourself a very cool nickname, what would it be? Why?

YEAR 1:

YEAR 2:

MARCH 3: What is the nastiest thing on the school cafeteria's menu?

NIKKI'S ANSWER: Umm . . . EVERYTHING?! But seriously, the worst would be sardine-and-cheese casserole, 'cause my stomach makes funny noises all day after I eat it.

YEAR 1:

YEAR 2:

MARCH 4: You're a world-famous SUPERSTAR! What's the BEST thing about being YOU? What's the WORST?

YEAR 1:

YEAR 2:

MARCH 5: What was the last thing you dreamed about?

YEAR 1:

YEAR 2:

MARCH 6: Your grandma just offered to buy you a new wardrobe. SQUEEE! List your favorite places to shop till you drop.

YEAR 1:

YEAR 2:

MARCH 7: You have a MAGICAL cell phone! It can call anyone, present or past. WHO would you call and why?

YEAR 1:

YEAR 2:

MARCH 8: What's the nicest thing someone has done for you lately? How did it make you feel?

YEAR 1:

YEAR 2:

MARCH 9: What personal accomplishment are you the most proud of?

YEAR 1:

YEAR 2:

MARCH 10: What's your favorite perfume or body spray? What does it smell like?

YEAR 1: The victoria secret one (it's pink) it's smells like blossoms.

YEAR 2:

MARCH 11: List the five most important traits of a BFF.

NIKKI'S ANSWER: To me, a good BFF . . .

1. gives you a big bear hug when you're down
2. shares their popcorn with you at the movies
3. keeps your crush TOP SECRET
4. helps you with tricky homework questions
5. supports you, even when they think you're crazy

YEAR 1: 1. honest to you 2. helps you when you're sad 3. supports you when your crazy 4. tells you most of the secrets. 5. loves you for you.

YEAR 2:

MARCH 12: Who is your FAVE teacher and why?

YEAR 1: Ms. Burrows, Ms. Thisqven, Mrs. Freitas, & Ms. Luupham because they are nice! :)

YEAR 2:

MARCH 13: What music fits your mood today: perky pop music, moody emo, or hyper hip-hop?

YEAR 1: POP music

YEAR 2:

MARCH 14: What song do you like to sing in the shower?

NIKKI'S ANSWER: The song from the Princess Sugar Plum cereal commercial. I hate it, but it's so catchy it gets stuck in my head!

YEAR 1: All of Me By John green ♡

YEAR 2:

MARCH 15: What was the last song that got stuck in YOUR head?

YEAR 1: idk, You & I? OR Problem.

YEAR 2:

MARCH 16: What yummy snack food do you crave most often?

YEAR 1: Chips, probably!

YEAR 2:

MARCH 17: HAPPY ST. PATRICK'S DAY! You just found a POT OF GOLD at the end of the rainbow. What are you going to do with it?

YEAR 1: give it to my family :)

YEAR 2:

MARCH 18: Who's your FAVE female celebrity and why?

YEAR 1: Ariana Grande: She's really nice! ♡
Selena G: She's inspirational! ♡
Katy Perry: She's a very kind person ♥ !!
& so much
MORE!

YEAR 2:

MARCH 19: Who's your FAVE male celebrity and why?

YEAR 1: So many! 1D♡ & they
are inspirational!!

YEAR 2:

MARCH 20: What thing do you like to doodle OBSESSIVELY? Doodle it in the space below.

YEAR 1:

idk why!
motavators hearts

YEAR 2:

MARCH 21: What was the last book you read that was SO good you didn't want it to end? Why did you like it?

YEAR 1:

YEAR 2:

MARCH 22: I LOVE SUPERcute shoes! What's YOUR fashion ADDICTION?

YEAR 1:

YEAR 2:

MARCH 23: Describe the home of your DREAMS. Where is it located?

YEAR 1:

YEAR 2:

MARCH 24: "I feel like a big baby when ________!"

YEAR 1: im afraid of stuff that everyone's not. (ㅠ)

YEAR 2:

MARCH 25: "I feel like a mature teen when ________!"

YEAR 1: I take care of children ♡

YEAR 2:

MARCH 26: List THREE things that you're SCARED TO DEATH to do but are SO going to try anyway.

YEAR 1: 1. Sky Dive!!
2. go on a Ship
3. & idk!!

YEAR 2:

MARCH 27: What fabulous birthday gift would make YOU totally FREAK OUT?

YEAR 1: Bethany Mota ♡

YEAR 2:

MARCH 28: What's your WEIRDEST habit?

NIKKI'S ANSWER: I talk in my sleep! A LOT!

YEAR 1: Uhm. i open my eyes when i sleep. kinda.

YEAR 2:

MARCH 29: Lately, have you been a NEAT FREAK or a PACK RAT?

YEAR 1: eh. Both?

YEAR 2:

MARCH 30: If you could be any Disney princess, which one would you choose and why?

YEAR 1: Definetly Cinderella. She's the BOMB!!! :) ♡

YEAR 2:

MARCH 31: Congratulations, PRINCESS! Today is your wedding day! Which Disney PRINCE are you going to marry and why?

YEAR 1: None. BCS forever ALONE.

YEAR 2:

APRIL

APRIL 1: HAPPY APRIL FOOL'S DAY! Did you prank anyone? Did anyone prank you? Details, please.

YEAR 1: No. and No.

YEAR 2:

APRIL 2: If you could go back in time, what AWESOME day would you like to relive?

YEAR 1: OMG! my old B-days ☹ & Beth's meet & greet!

YEAR 2:

APRIL 3: If you could go back in time, what CRUDDY day would you like to fix?

YEAR 1: idk. a lot of Days!

YEAR 2:

APRIL 4: April showers bring May flowers! What do YOU like to do on a rainy day?

YEAR 1: Stay home . . .

YEAR 2:

APRIL 5: We just gave your BEDROOM an EXTREME MAKEOVER! Describe what it looks like!

YEAR 1: Blue. with the word Motavator & Bethany Mota ♡

YEAR 2:

APRIL 6: What's the last thing you were grounded for?

NIKKI'S ANSWER: My paint smock was in the washing machine, so I borrowed one of my dad's work shirts and accidentally dropped a huge blob of turquoise paint on it. He wore it to work the next day! To be honest . . . I think the extra hint of color really brought out the blue in his eyes.

YEAR 1: Oh. IDK.

YEAR 2:

APRIL 7: Describe a time you helped out someone with a problem. How did it make you feel?

YEAR 1: i saved someone from getting hit by a basketball. I felt like a hero!! :)

YEAR 2:

APRIL 8: I'm totally OBSESSED with ART!! What activity are YOU totally obsessed with?

YEAR 1: ART. And fangirling over Beth

YEAR 2:

APRIL 9: SMART, CUTE, or FUNNY? What characteristic in a CRUSH gives you RCS?

YEAR 1: Ugly. BCS i don't have a CRUSh.

YEAR 2:

APRIL 10: Everyone has a HIDDEN talent! What's YOURS?

YEAR 1: nothing . . .

YEAR 2:

APRIL 11: "I always feel REALLY overwhelmed when ________." Fill in the blank and state why.

YEAR 1:

YEAR 2:

APRIL 12: What's your HARDEST subject in school? What's your EASIEST subject in school?

YEAR 1: Hardest: Math; ew (ugly handwriting
easiest: Lunch :) kill me!

YEAR 2:

APRIL 13: "I've been wanting to take ____________ lessons, like . . . FOREVER!!" Explain why.

YEAR 1:

YEAR 2:

APRIL 14: What type of candy would you love to munch on right now? List your three favorites.

YEAR 1:

YEAR 2:

APRIL 15: You and I have A LOT of things in common! List them below.

YEAR 1:

YEAR 2:

APRIL 16: If you could be on the cover of ANY magazine, which would it be and why?

YEAR 1:

YEAR 2:

APRIL 17: What's something you can do now that you couldn't do last year?

YEAR 1:

YEAR 2:

APRIL 18: If you could create a holiday, what would it be called, and how would you celebrate it?

NIKKI'S ANSWER: My holiday would be called National Dork Day! We'd have a big carnival at school and appreciate the things that make us unique!

YEAR 1:

YEAR 2:

APRIL 19: What toppings do you love on your pizza?

YEAR 1:

YEAR 2:

APRIL 20: It's right around Easter time! Take time out to count your blessings! List them below.

YEAR 1:

YEAR 2:

APRIL 21: What's your FAVORITE movie of all time? Why?

YEAR 1:

YEAR 2:

APRIL 22: What's your favorite ROMANTIC movie? Why?

YEAR 1:

YEAR 2:

APRIL 23: YOU just gave ME a GLAM makeover! Describe my FAB hairstyle and CHIC outfit!

YEAR 1:

YEAR 2:

APRIL 24: I just gave YOU a GLAM makeover! Describe your FAB new hairstyle and your CHIC outfit!

YEAR 1:

YEAR 2:

APRIL 25: Name as many balls (example: "basketball") as you can in the space below. Then circle your favorite ball and cross out your least favorite.

YEAR 1:

YEAR 2:

APRIL 26: Do you remember a time you were SO HAPPY you wanted to CRY? Details, please.

I won first place in the WCD art show!

YEAR 1:

YEAR 2:

APRIL 27: Choose ONE word to describe yourself. Why this word?

YEAR 1:

YEAR 2:

APRIL 28: Choose ONE word to describe your BFF. Why this word?

YEAR 1:

YEAR 2:

APRIL 29: You're dining out with your family! LOVE the quality time or EMBARRASSED that kids from school will see you with them?

YEAR 1:

YEAR 2:

APRIL 30: You went a little crazy at the pet store! Come up with cute names for your four new pets: Dog? Cat? Goldfish? Monkey?

YEAR 1:

YEAR 2:

MAY

MAY 1: OMG! You're working at a KISSING BOOTH to raise money for CHARITY! Name the first six people in line for kisses!

YEAR 1:

YEAR 2:

MAY 2: What personal item do you own that is PRICELESS? Why is it so valuable?

NIKKI'S ANSWER: My diary is priceless! It's like a BFF in book form. I'd probably have a meltdown if I ever lost it.

YEAR 1:

YEAR 2:

MAY 3: "I am SO over ______________!" Fill in the blank and state why.

YEAR 1:

YEAR 2:

MAY 4: If your life were a book, what would the title be and why?

YEAR 1:

YEAR 2:

MAY 5: "I'd clean the house for a month if only my parents would let me ______________!"

YEAR 1:

YEAR 2:

MAY 6: MOTHER'S DAY is just around the corner! List FIVE reasons why YOUR mom is the BEST mother EVER! Now make a Mother's Day card for her with this special note written inside.

YEAR 1:

YEAR 2:

MAY 7: If you could have any animal as a pet, what would it be and why?

YEAR 1:

YEAR 2:

MAY 8: You and your BFFs are playing TRUTH OR DARE! Which one do you pick and why?

YEAR 1:

YEAR 2:

MAY 9: What TRUTH would you dread most? What DARE would you dread most?

YEAR 1:

YEAR 2:

MAY 10: YOU just launched a FAB new fashion line for tween girls! Describe what your clothing line looks like.

YEAR 1:

YEAR 2:

MAY 11: Your parents have a chat with your teacher about your progress in class. Are you as cool as a cucumber or sweating bullets?

YEAR 1:

YEAR 2:

MAY 12: Would you rather travel by plane, train, or boat? Why?

YEAR 1:

YEAR 2:

MAY 13: You just totally BLINGED out your locker at school! What does it look like?

YEAR 1:

YEAR 2:

MAY 14: Do you carefully plan out your day or just go with the flow? Why?

YEAR 1:

YEAR 2:

MAY 15: You and your BFFs are planning the most AWESOME one-week vacation EVER! Details, please.

YEAR 1:

YEAR 2:

MAY 16: Make a list of the things in your backpack or purse. Circle the most important thing. Cross out the least important thing.

YEAR 1:

YEAR 2:

MAY 17: WHO do you miss most when they're not around and why?

YEAR 1:

YEAR 2:

MAY 18: What's the worst gift you've ever received?

NIKKI'S ANSWER: For Christmas, I got five-sizes-too-large work boots from my neighbor, Mrs. Wallabanger. And she gave my dad a pair of pink sequined Uggs that were way too small. I think she accidentally switched our presents!

YEAR 1:

YEAR 2:

MAY 19: Are you a dog person or a cat person? Why?

YEAR 1:

YEAR 2:

MAY 20: What family activity makes you feel warm and fuzzy inside?

YEAR 1:

YEAR 2:

MAY 21: What family activity do you HATE so much you'd rather chew tinfoil?

YEAR 1:

YEAR 2:

MAY 22: Would you rather spend the day floating UNDER the sea or ABOVE the clouds?

YEAR 1:

YEAR 2:

MAY 23: Who should win the Coolest Teacher of the Year award at your school and why?

YEAR 1:

YEAR 2:

MAY 24: What do you hope will happen by the end of the school year and why?

YEAR 1:

YEAR 2:

MAY 25: What's the KLUTZIEST thing you've done in public lately?

YEAR 1:

YEAR 2:

MAY 26: Describe a time you had a problem with a friend and made things right.

YEAR 1:

YEAR 2:

MAY 27: The term "GGG" means "giggling, gossiping, and glossing." Which of these are you the most guilty of doing?

YEAR 1:

YEAR 2:

MAY 28: You're spending a day at the beach! What's the first thing you plan to do: chillax with music, build a huge sand castle, or go for a swim?

YEAR 1:

YEAR 2:

MAY 29: Name your three best qualities.

NIKKI'S ANSWER:

1. I'm very DORKY!
2. I've got a wacky sense of humor.
3. I'm a pretty good artist.

YEAR 1:

YEAR 2:

MAY 30: It's raining and you're stuck inside! What three video games would you like to play?

YEAR 1:

YEAR 2:

MAY 31: Describe your most romantic fantasy date! Details, please!

YEAR 1:

YEAR 2:

JUNE

JUNE 1: Your teacher is making you watch a SUPERlong, SUPERboring documentary about SLUGS! EWW! Do you force yourself to pay attention, do you doodle in your notebook, or do you fall asleep?

YEAR 1:

YEAR 2:

JUNE 2: What was the best compliment you've received lately? How did it make you feel?

YEAR 1:

YEAR 2:

JUNE 3: Name someone you know who's smart and loves to read, like my BFF Zoey.

YEAR 1:

YEAR 2:

JUNE 4: Name someone you know who's a HOPELESS ROMANTIC and BOY CRAZY, like my BFF Chloe.

YEAR 1:

YEAR 2:

JUNE 5: What makes you really hyper?

NIKKI'S ANSWER: Whenever Mom takes me to the art store to get new colored pencils, paints, and stuff, I get really excited and hyper, like Brianna in a candy shop.

YEAR 1:

YEAR 2:

JUNE 6: What makes you totally exhausted?

YEAR 1:

YEAR 2:

JUNE 7: You just started a band with six of your friends! What is your band called, and who does what in it?

YEAR 1:

YEAR 2:

JUNE 8: What color nail polish best fits your mood right now? Give it a cool name.

YEAR 1:

YEAR 2:

JUNE 9: Congratulations! You just won the Nobel Peace Prize for making the world a better place. What did you do to get it?

YEAR 1:

YEAR 2:

JUNE 10: FINALLY! School's out for the summer!! What do you plan to do your first week at home? Make a short list.

YEAR 1:

YEAR 2:

JUNE 11: "I used to think ______________
was totally LAME, but now think it's really COOL!"

YEAR 1:

YEAR 2:

JUNE 12: "I used to think ______________
was really COOL, but now think it's totally LAME!"

YEAR 1:

YEAR 2:

JUNE 13: You just started a dance crew that performs at local events! Who is in it? Give your group a cool name, like Dorkalicious!

YEAR 1:

YEAR 2:

JUNE 14: FATHER'S DAY is just around the corner! List FIVE reasons why YOUR dad is the BEST father EVER! Now make a Father's Day card for him with this special note written inside.

YEAR 1:

YEAR 2:

JUNE 15: My friend Zoey has a famous quote for every occasion. What was the last really deep thing a friend said that totally blew your mind?

YEAR 1:

YEAR 2:

JUNE 16: WHO or WHAT do you FEAR as much as Brianna fears the tooth fairy?

YEAR 1:

YEAR 2:

JUNE 17: What makes you wanna throw up in your mouth a little?

NIKKI'S ANSWER: Watching my sister, Brianna, eat her favorite snack: a ketchup-and-banana sandwich. EWW!!!

YEAR 1:

YEAR 2:

JUNE 18: What's the most awesome party you've been to this year? What made it so special?

YEAR 1:

YEAR 2:

JUNE 19: You're a SUPERfamous celebrity! Are you a singer, actress, supermodel, athlete, or something else? Explain.

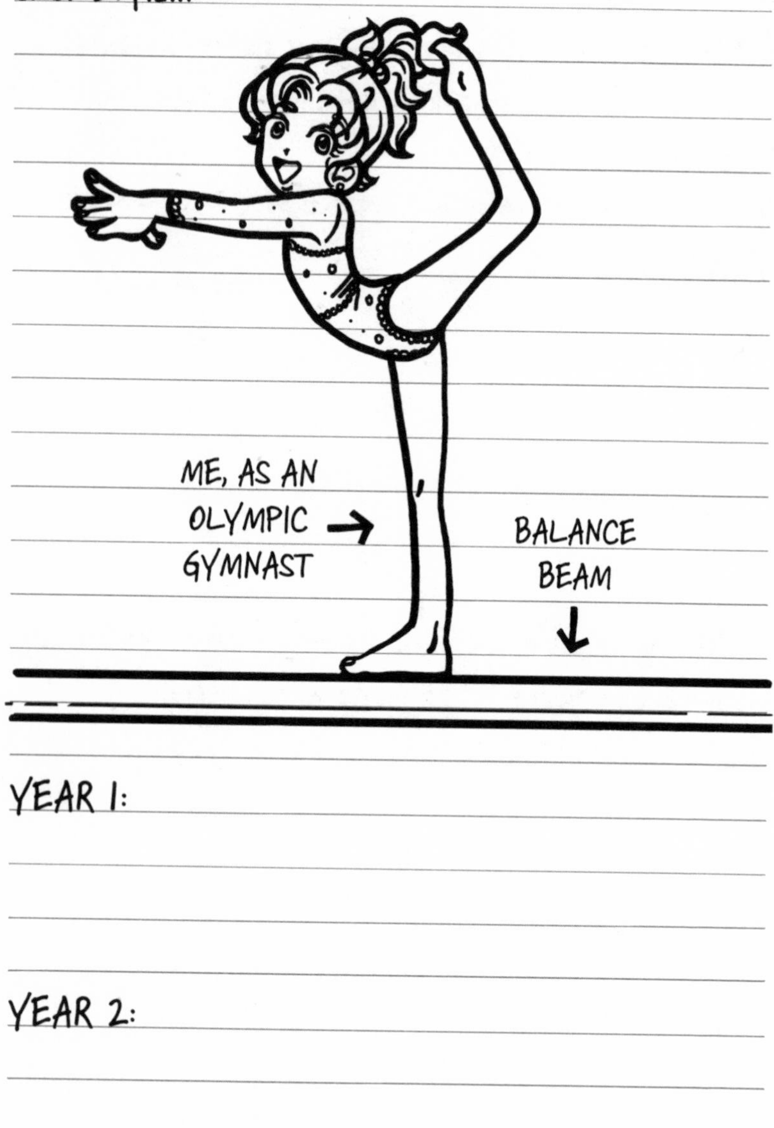

YEAR 1:

YEAR 2:

JUNE 20: What do you look forward to most about getting older: attending high school, driving a car, dating, getting a part-time job, or something else? Explain.

YEAR 1:

YEAR 2:

JUNE 21: Do you have more fun hanging out at the mall with your seven closest friends or chilling in your room with your BFFs?

NIKKI'S ANSWER: Chilling in my room with Chloe and Zoey, of course ☺!

YEAR 1:

YEAR 2:

JUNE 22: OMG! Your annoying little sister just stole your diary! How do you plan to get it back?

YEAR 1:

YEAR 2:

JUNE 23: When was the last time you tattled on your brother or sister? Explain what happened.

YEAR 1:

YEAR 2:

JUNE 24: When was the last time your brother or sister tattled on you? Explain what happened.

YEAR 1:

YEAR 2:

JUNE 25: WOW! You have a video on YouTube with 1 million views! What are you doing in it?

YEAR 1:

YEAR 2:

JUNE 26: If you could be any age right now, what would it be and why?

YEAR 1:

YEAR 2:

JUNE 27: Today Chloe, Zoey, and I will be hanging out at YOUR house! SQUEEE! What are we going to do together? Plan a SUPERfun day!

YEAR 1:

YEAR 2:

JUNE 28: If you could create your very own DREAM summer camp, what would it be called? Describe it.

YEAR 1:

YEAR 2:

JUNE 29: Make a list of the stuff you'll bring to your dream camp so you and your bunkmates will have a ton of fun!

YEAR 1:

YEAR 2:

JUNE 30: You just landed your very own reality show starring YOU and your BFFs! What is it called? What is it about? Who are your other costars?

YEAR 1:

YEAR 2:

JULY

JULY 1: It's ninety-two degrees outside! Would you rather spend the day splashing around at the BEACH or the WATER PARK?

YEAR 1:

YEAR 2:

JULY 2: What is the one thing a family member does that DRIVES YOU NUTS?!!!

NIKKI'S ANSWER: Brianna likes to drive me crazy by letting Miss Penelope "taste test" my food. One time Brianna dunked her entire hand in my spaghetti! EWW! It was SOOO gross!!

YEAR 1:

YEAR 2:

JULY 3: "OMG! I can hardly wait until ________!!"

YEAR 1:

YEAR 2:

JULY 4: HAPPY FOURTH OF JULY! Which do you enjoy most? Sitting in the dark watching FIREWORKS or running around in the dark with SPARKLERS?

YEAR 1:

YEAR 2:

JULY 5: There's a 50% OFF sale at the mall! List five things you need to add to your summer wardrobe to kick it up a notch.

YEAR 1:

YEAR 2:

JULY 6: You discover a dusty time-travel machine in your attic! Are you going to travel into the PAST or the FUTURE? Where do you decide to go and why?

YEAR 1:

YEAR 2:

JULY 7: You need CASH for a concert ticket . . . and QUICK! Do you become the neighborhood dog walker? Open a lemonade stand? Or set up a girl-powered car wash?

YEAR 1:

YEAR 2:

JULY 8: Which celebrity are you SO sick of, you'd like to send him/her on a one-way trip to Mars? Why?

YEAR 1:

YEAR 2:

JULY 9: What was the last thing your mom or dad did that was SO embarrassing, you wanted to take out a newspaper ad that read "Teen Girl Seeking NEW PARENTS! No experience necessary!"

YEAR 1:

YEAR 2:

JULY 10: You just landed the BEST summer job EVER! What are you doing?

YEAR 1:

YEAR 2:

JULY 11: You just got stuck with the WORST summer job EVER! What are you doing?

NIKKI'S ANSWER: I'd feel REALLY sorry for anyone who has to babysit Brianna! Wait a minute—that IS my summer job ☹!!

YEAR 1:

YEAR 2:

JULY 12: You just earned your wings as a fairy godmother! To WHOM would you grant three wishes and why?

YEAR 1:

YEAR 2:

JULY 13: What was the last movie you saw that SCARED you so badly you had to sleep with the lights on?

YEAR 1:

YEAR 2:

JULY 14: What's your FAVE ice cream flavor?

NIKKI'S ANSWER: Birthday-cake-flavored ice cream with confetti sprinkles! YUMMY!

YEAR 1:

YEAR 2:

JULY 15: "I would have a complete MELTDOWN if ____________."

YEAR 1:

YEAR 2:

JULY 16: If you were going to be stranded on a desert island for two days, what three things would you bring with you (other than food and water)?

YEAR 1:

YEAR 2:

JULY 17: OOPS! You're in trouble with your parents! Which punishment do you most DREAD? No TV for a week, no cell phone for a week, or no leaving the house for a week?

YEAR 1:

YEAR 2:

JULY 18: "My favorite song of the summer is ________."

YEAR 1:

YEAR 2:

JULY 19: Describe a time you tried really hard to do something special, but it didn't quite turn out the way you had planned.

YEAR 1:

YEAR 2:

JULY 20: What do you daydream about?

YEAR 1:

YEAR 2:

JULY 21: Your dad just announced that your family will be spending some quality time together in the wilderness! Would you rather stay in a TENT, a CABIN, or an RV (recreational vehicle) and why?

YEAR 1:

YEAR 2:

JULY 22: You just got your driver's license! SQUEEE!! Describe the dream car you'll be driving to school every day.

YEAR 1:

YEAR 2:

JULY 23: OMG! You just found a can of MAGICAL repellent. Name three things you'd love to spray to make them magically go away.

NIKKI'S ANSWER: MacKenzie! Just kidding ☺!

YEAR 1:

YEAR 2:

JULY 24: What do you want to be when you grow up and why?

YEAR 1:

YEAR 2:

JULY 25: What was the last movie you saw that made you cry your eyes out?

YEAR 1:

YEAR 2:

JULY 26: What book would you LOVE to see turned into a movie?

NIKKI'S ANSWER: Um . . . I think you already know MY answer: DORK DIARIES!

YEAR 1:

YEAR 2:

JULY 27: What recent family activity turned into a COMPLETE DISASTER?!

YEAR 1:

YEAR 2:

JULY 28: Are you an early bird or a night owl?

YEAR 1:

YEAR 2:

JULY 29: What TV show is so bad you wish it would just get canceled already?

YEAR 1:

YEAR 2:

JULY 30: You're going to a formal dance and want to be the belle of the ball. What kind of dress will you wear?

A) Something pink, soft, and delicate that's fit for a princess!

B) Something black, shimmery, and mysterious that will turn heads!

C) Something bright, bold, and fun that will stand out from the crowd!

YEAR 1:

YEAR 2:

JULY 31: You're building your very own amusement park! Describe what it looks like and the types of rides you have, and give your park a name.

YEAR 1:

YEAR 2:

AUGUST

AUGUST 1: Do you have a collection of anything? What is it and how many do you have? Why do you collect them?

YEAR 1:

YEAR 2:

AUGUST 2: Your dad is outside cooking on his grill! Do you ask for a hot dog, a hamburger, a steak, or grilled veggies?

NIKKI'S ANSWER: My dad is HORRIBLE at grilling and usually burns everything to a CRISP. So I ask for McDonald's ☺! Sorry, Dad!

YEAR 1:

YEAR 2:

AUGUST 3: If given the chance, would you be like Peter Pan and stay a KID forever? Why or why not?

YEAR 1:

YEAR 2:

AUGUST 4: Which friend could you talk to for hours and never get bored?

YEAR 1:

YEAR 2:

AUGUST 5: "Okay, I'll admit it! The thing that makes my MOM kind of cool is ______________!"

YEAR 1:

YEAR 2:

AUGUST 6: "Okay, I'll admit it! The thing that makes my DAD kind of cool is ______________!"

YEAR 1:

YEAR 2:

AUGUST 7: What's something you've just recently learned about your BFF?

CHLOE SOMETIMES WEARS GLASSES?!!

YEAR 1:

YEAR 2:

AUGUST 8: Imagine you and your crush were a celebrity couple. Combine your names together and make yourselves a cute Hollywood nickname!

NIKKI'S ANSWER: Okay, for Brandon and me, how about . . . BRANNIK! SQUEEEE ☺!!

YEAR 1:

YEAR 2:

AUGUST 9: What is your favorite smell and why?

NIKKI'S ANSWER: I LOVE the smell of cookies baking in the oven. Mostly because it means I get to EAT them ☺!

YEAR 1:

YEAR 2:

AUGUST 10: If you could have a superhero power, what would it be and why? What would be your superhero name?

YEAR 1:

YEAR 2:

AUGUST 11: Which cute celebrity would be a good match for Chloe?

YEAR 1:

YEAR 2:

AUGUST 12: Which cute celebrity would be a good match for Zoey?

YEAR 1:

YEAR 2:

AUGUST 13: What do YOU think is the WORST pet EVER?!

YEAR 1:

YEAR 2:

AUGUST 14: If you could spend a week anywhere in the entire WORLD, where would you go and why?

YEAR 1:

YEAR 2:

AUGUST 15: You want a friend's opinion on your new hairstyle. Do you want him/her to be brutally honest with you or careful not to hurt your feelings?

YEAR 1:

YEAR 2:

AUGUST 16: What's your favorite board game and why? Who do you like to play it with?

YEAR 1:

YEAR 2:

AUGUST 17: If you could change anything about yourself, what would it be and why?

YEAR 1:

YEAR 2:

AUGUST 18: What's something you've RECENTLY changed about yourself for the better?

NIKKI'S ANSWER: I've learned how to stand up to mean girls like MacKenzie.

YEAR 1:

YEAR 2:

AUGUST 19: You're on the show *America's Next Top Model*, and Tyra wants to cut your hair into a short 'n' funky style. Do you say YES and enjoy your chic new look, or NO WAY and agree to be sent home?

YEAR 1:

YEAR 2:

AUGUST 20: If you were an inventor, what awesome new gadget would you come up with? What does it do?

YEAR 1:

YEAR 2:

AUGUST 21: If you had a hand puppet friend like Miss Penelope, what would you name him/her? Describe his/her personality.

YEAR 1:

YEAR 2:

AUGUST 22: Draw a picture of YOUR hand puppet friend below by adding silly-looking eyes, lashes, lips, hair, etc. Have fun!

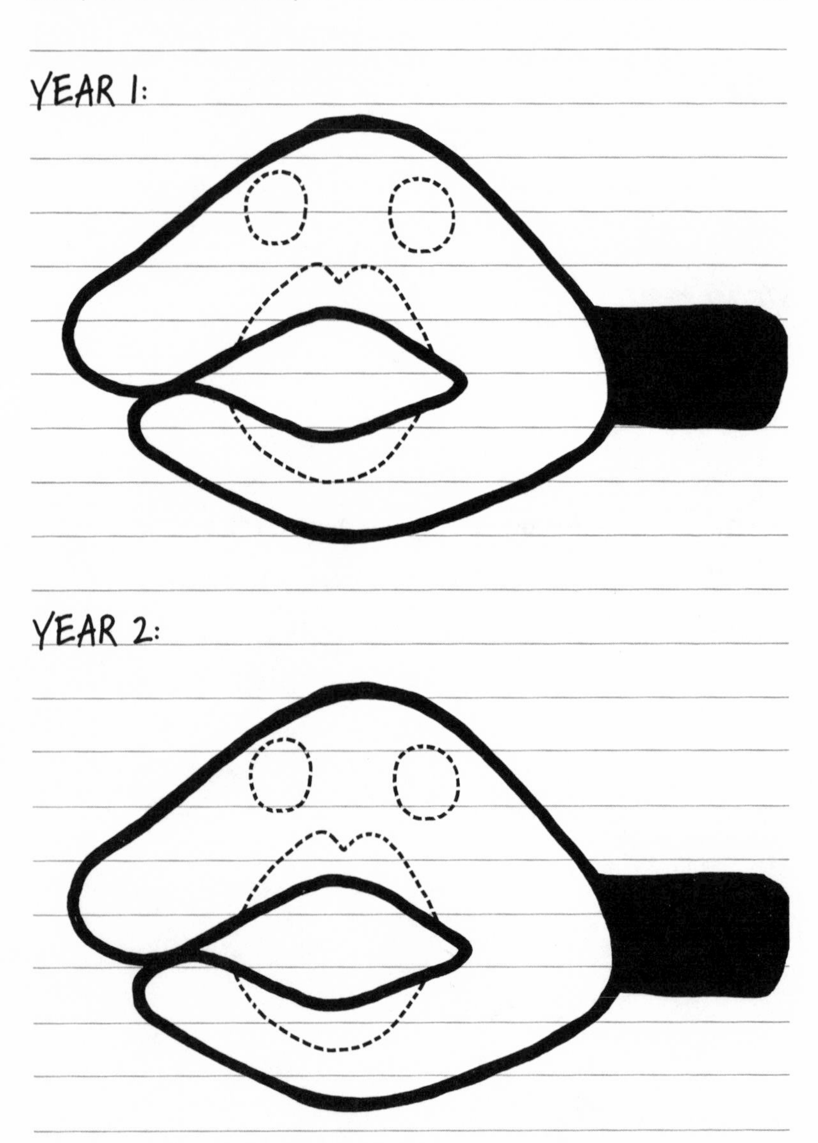

AUGUST 23: Your summer vacation is almost over. Did it ZOOM by SUPERfast or DRAG on and on FOREVER? Explain.

YEAR 1:

YEAR 2:

AUGUST 24: "I'm going to SCREAM if I hear someone use the slang word or phrase ______________ AGAIN!! ☹!"

NIKKI'S ANSWER: Yes, I know! I use the slang word "OMG!" WAAAAAAY too much!!

YEAR 1:

YEAR 2:

AUGUST 25: If you could put your favorite motto or saying on a T-shirt, what would it say?

YEAR 1:

YEAR 2:

AUGUST 26: What's something you HATE doing so much you wait until the very last minute to do it?

YEAR 1:

YEAR 2:

AUGUST 27: If you could be a character in any book, who would it be and why?

YEAR 1:

YEAR 2:

AUGUST 28: Name three household chores that you absolutely DETEST. State why for each.

YEAR 1:

YEAR 2:

AUGUST 29: "I'm a little WORRIED about starting my next year in school because ______________."

YEAR 1:

YEAR 2:

AUGUST 30: "I'm superEXCITED about starting my next year in school because ______________."

YEAR 1:

YEAR 2:

AUGUST 31: "I'll NEVER forget how much FUN I had this summer when I ________________ ☺!" Draw a picture below.

YEAR 1:

YEAR 2:

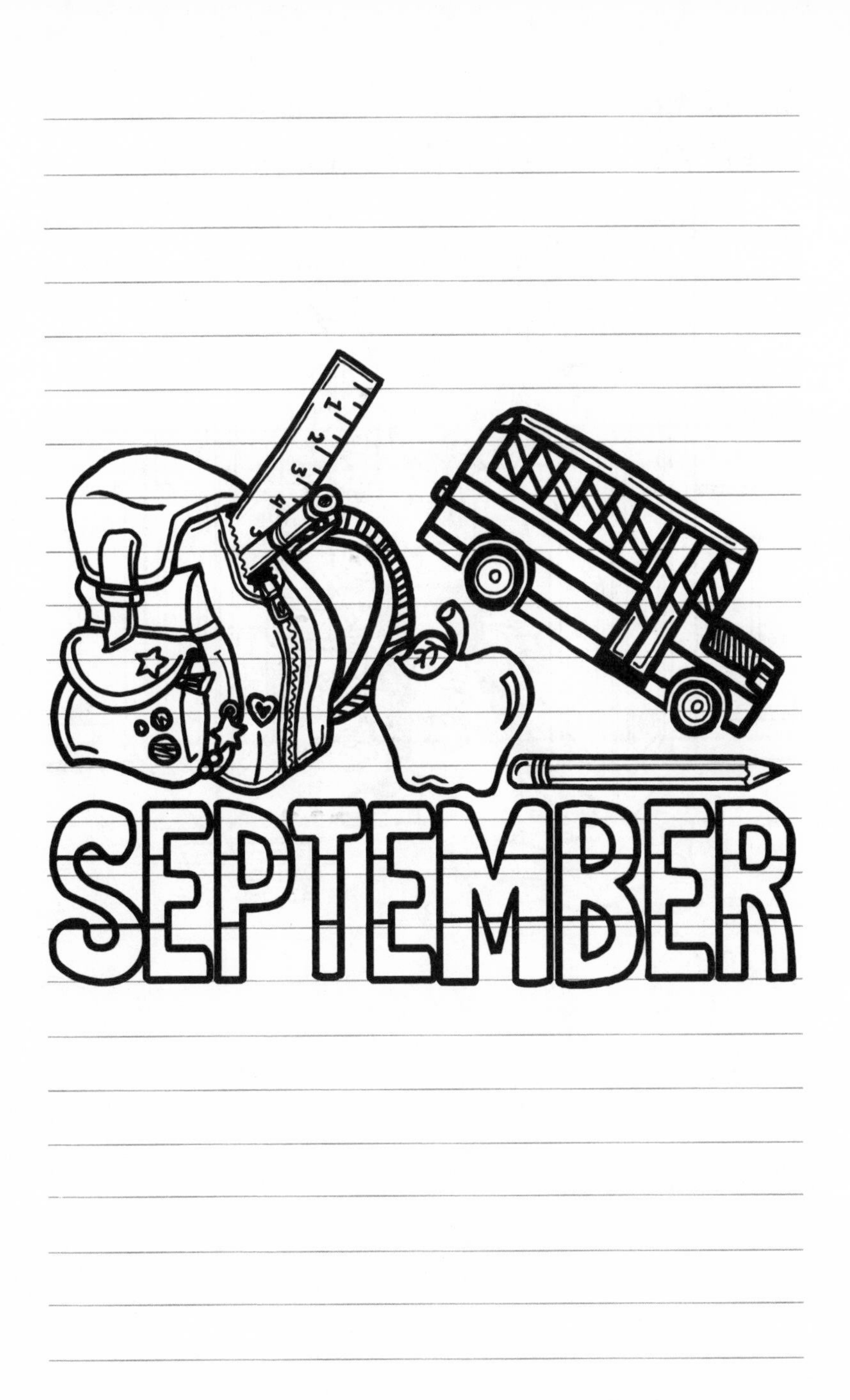

1 2 3 4 5
SEPTEMBER

SEPTEMBER 1: What's your first-day-of-school outfit? Also list your outfits for the rest of the week.

YEAR 1:

YEAR 2:

SEPTEMBER 2: You're about to select a desk in your brand-new classroom. Do you sit in the front, middle, or back row and why?

YEAR 1:

YEAR 2:

SEPTEMBER 3: Who are your top three favorite movie heroines and why?

YEAR 1:

YEAR 2:

SEPTEMBER 4: If your school cafeteria was actually a restaurant, how many stars would you give it and why? Rate it with one to five stars (five stars being the best).

YEAR 1:

YEAR 2:

SEPTEMBER 5: The head cook at your school just asked for your help making a yummy lunch menu students will LOVE! What do you suggest?

YEAR 1:

YEAR 2:

SEPTEMBER 6: If you could perform in the school talent show, what would you do? Details, please.

NIKKI'S ANSWER: I'd perform a song that I wrote with my band, Dorkalicious, also known as Actually, I'm Not Really Sure Yet!

YEAR 1:

YEAR 2:

SEPTEMBER 7: Today you have your checkup with your DENTIST! Are you cool as a cucumber or sweating bullets? Explain.

YEAR 1:

YEAR 2:

SEPTEMBER 8: If you had to work at your school, would you rather be a TEACHER or the PRINCIPAL? Why?

YEAR 1:

YEAR 2:

SEPTEMBER 9: If you were a teacher, would you rather teach at an elementary school, a middle school, or a high school? Explain.

YEAR 1:

YEAR 2:

SEPTEMBER 10: Your mom just fixed the most delish breakfast EVER! Are you eating a syrup-covered stack of PANCAKES, WAFFLES, or FRENCH TOAST?

YEAR 1:

YEAR 2:

SEPTEMBER 11: What's your fave subject in school and why?

YEAR 1:

YEAR 2:

SEPTEMBER 12: What's your least fave subject in school and why?

YEAR 1:

YEAR 2:

SEPTEMBER 13: You finally managed to save up a hundred dollars from your babysitting jobs! What are you going to do with it?

YEAR 1:

YEAR 2:

SEPTEMBER 14: Who is your NEWEST friend?

NIKKI'S ANSWER: My newest friend is Marcy. I met her when I joined the school newspaper.

YEAR 1:

YEAR 2:

SEPTEMBER 15: Which friend have you known, like, FOREVER?

YEAR 1:

YEAR 2:

SEPTEMBER 16: What do you wish you were doing right now?

YEAR 1:

YEAR 2:

SEPTEMBER 17: "The most AWESOME thing about my life right now is ________________!"

YEAR 1:

YEAR 2:

SEPTEMBER 18: "The most CRUDDY thing about my life right now is ________________!"

YEAR 1:

YEAR 2:

SEPTEMBER 19: Theodore L. Swagmire III is my dorkiest guy friend. Who is YOUR dorkiest guy friend?

YEAR 1:

YEAR 2:

SEPTEMBER 20: Which of your friends reminds you most of Chloe?

YEAR 1:

YEAR 2:

SEPTEMBER 21: Which of your friends reminds you most of Zoey?

YEAR 1:

YEAR 2:

SEPTEMBER 22: What girl at your school reminds you most of MacKenzie?

YEAR 1:

YEAR 2:

SEPTEMBER 23: "MacKenzie would be a much nicer person if only she would ______________."

YEAR 1:

YEAR 2:

SEPTEMBER 24: What thing does your mom or dad say over and over again like a broken record?

NIKKI'S ANSWER: If they say "Young lady, I expect you to be a good role model for your sister!" one more time, I'm going to SCREAM!

YEAR 1:

YEAR 2:

SEPTEMBER 25: Has anyone ever done something to you "accidentally on purpose"? Explain what happened.

YEAR 1:

YEAR 2:

SEPTEMBER 26: Who's the funniest kid you know? What was the last thing he/she did to make you laugh?

NIKKI'S ANSWER: Sometimes Chloe is such a clown! Whenever she does jazz hands, I totally crack up.

YEAR 1:

YEAR 2:

SEPTEMBER 27: What kid at your school would you like to become better friends with? Why?

YEAR 1:

YEAR 2:

SEPTEMBER 28: It's picture day, and you have a zit the size of a small grape! YIKES! What are you going to do?!!

YEAR 1:

YEAR 2:

SEPTEMBER 29: Would you rather be a cheerleader cheering for your team or an athlete playing in the game? Why?

YEAR 1:

YEAR 2:

SEPTEMBER 30: You're running for president of the student council! List five reasons why you'd be AWESOME in that position.

YEAR 1:

YEAR 2:

OCTOBER

OCTOBER 1: Who's the LAST person you'd want to be stuck in an elevator with?

YEAR 1:

YEAR 2:

OCTOBER 2: How would your friends describe you?

NIKKI'S ANSWER: They would say I'm friendly, funny, and a fantastic BFF!

YEAR 1:

YEAR 2:

OCTOBER 3: What cherished toy do you still SECRETLY play with whenever you can?

YEAR 1:

YEAR 2:

OCTOBER 4: Your dad just raked up a huge pile of leaves. Do you help pick them up or run and jump into the pile?

YEAR 1:

YEAR 2:

OCTOBER 5: What's the nicest thing you've done for someone lately?

NIKKI'S ANSWER: I surprised my sister, Brianna, with a batch of homemade cookies ☺!

YEAR 1:

YEAR 2:

OCTOBER 6: What's the nicest thing someone has done for YOU lately?

YEAR 1:

YEAR 2:

OCTOBER 7: You're ready to make some MUSIC! Do you join the marching band, orchestra, or glee club?

YEAR 1:

YEAR 2:

OCTOBER 8: What makes you feel SUPERinsecure?

YEAR 1:

YEAR 2:

OCTOBER 9: What gives you an instant boost of confidence?

NIKKI'S ANSWER: A group hug with my BFFs, Chloe and Zoey!

YEAR 1:

YEAR 2:

OCTOBER 10: You've decided to try out for a sports team! Which will it be?

YEAR 1:

YEAR 2:

OCTOBER 11: Are you an OPTIMIST or a PESSIMIST? What have you said or done lately that reflects this?

YEAR 1:

YEAR 2:

OCTOBER 12: MacKenzie is in a clique called the CCPs (Cute, Cool & Popular). Make up a cool name for your group of friends. Write the name and the initials below.

YEAR 1:

YEAR 2:

OCTOBER 13: What do you want to be for Halloween this year? Describe your costume in detail.

YEAR 1:

YEAR 2:

OCTOBER 14: OMG!! Your crush finally asks you to the Halloween dance! What do you do?

A) Grin from ear to ear and say, "Sure!"

B) Toss your hair with a sly smile and say, "Let me think about it and get back to you."

C) Scream, "AAAAAAAAH!!!" and go hide in the girls' bathroom

YEAR 1:

YEAR 2:

OCTOBER 15: You're going to the Halloween dance with your crush! SQUEEE! What costumes will you both wear as a couple?

YEAR 1:

YEAR 2:

OCTOBER 16: Who do you NOT get along with, no matter how hard you try? Explain.

YEAR 1:

YEAR 2:

OCTOBER 17: Your teacher has agreed to take your class on a field trip! Where do YOU want to go and why?

NIKKI'S ANSWER: The art museum. I LOVE art!

YEAR 1:

YEAR 2:

OCTOBER 18: Who was the last person to make you smile? Details, please.

YEAR 1:

YEAR 2:

OCTOBER 19: You just finished carving your pumpkin and have leftover PUMPKIN GUTS!!! EWW! Do you throw them away, throw them at someone, or throw up?

YEAR 1:

YEAR 2:

OCTOBER 20: Chloe, Zoey, and I need cool ideas for Halloween costumes! Please give each of us a suggestion.

YEAR 1:

YEAR 2:

OCTOBER 21: You're planning a big Halloween bash! Come up with a cool party theme with decorations. Who will you invite?

YEAR 1:

YEAR 2:

OCTOBER 22: I once wore a smelly rat costume to a Halloween party for Brianna's dance class. List three costumes that you think would be even more HIDEOUS!

YEAR 1:

YEAR 2:

OCTOBER 23: OMG! Your parents are dressed up as a chicken and an egg and are insisting on going trick-or-treating with you! What do you do?

A) Say, "No way!" and stay home

B) Say, "Okay," but ditch them at the first house

C) Join in on the fun and dress up as a farmer

NIKKI'S ANSWER: Ditch them at the first house! Just kidding ☺!

YEAR 1:

YEAR 2:

OCTOBER 24: "What I like MOST about the fall season is ____________! What I like LEAST about it is ____________!"

YEAR 1:

YEAR 2:

OCTOBER 25: Draw your very own jack-o'-lantern! You can make it happy, silly, or scary. Then, with your parents' permission, use this design to make a real one!

YEAR 1:

YEAR 2:

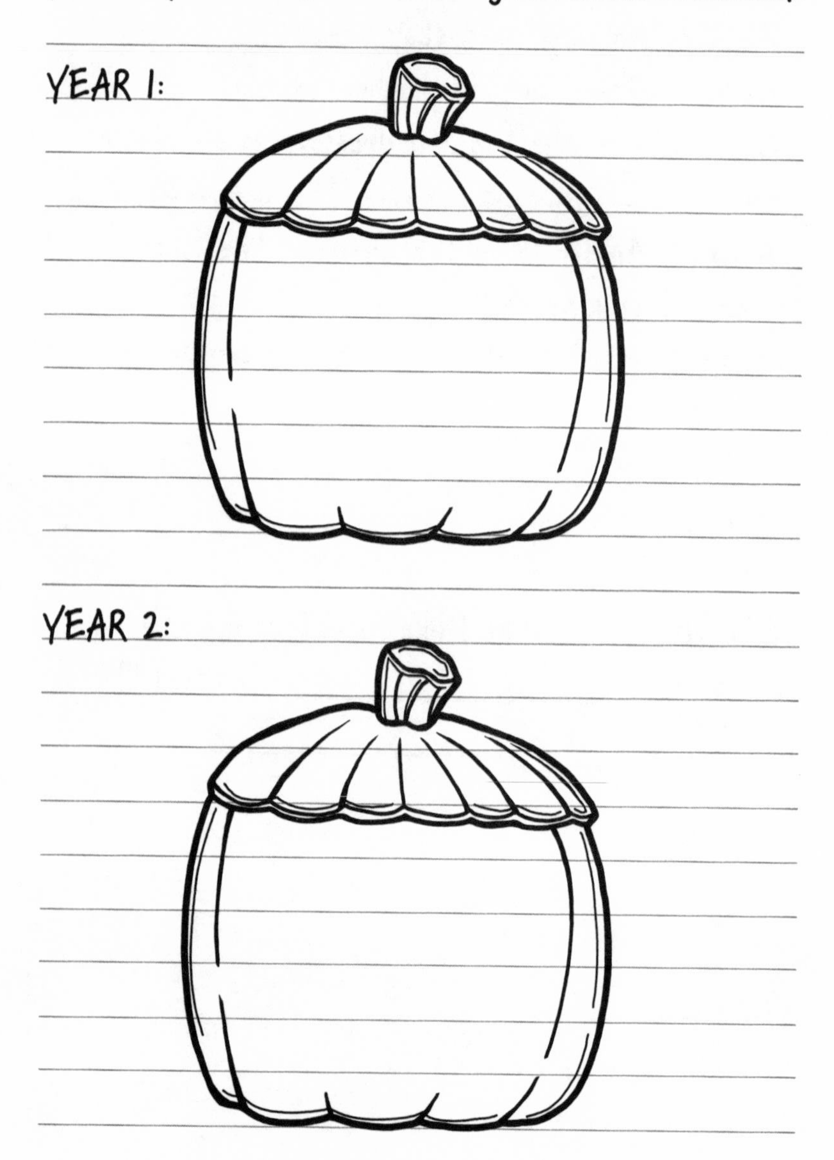

OCTOBER 26: What would be the perfect Halloween costume for MacKenzie?

NIKKI'S ANSWER: The Wicked Witch of the West, for sure ☺!

YEAR 1:

YEAR 2:

OCTOBER 27: "My favorite Halloween candy is ______! My least favorite Halloween candy is __________!"

YEAR 1:

YEAR 2:

OCTOBER 28: Your school is having a haunted house to raise money for a charity! What will you do to help scare your classmates out of their wits?

YEAR 1:

YEAR 2:

OCTOBER 29: Your magic crystal ball shows you what happens to Brandon and me in the future. What do you see? I'm DYING to know ☺!

YEAR 1:

YEAR 2:

OCTOBER 30: Your neighbor has a sign on a bowl of candy that says "Help yourself!" Do you take one piece, a handful, or all of it? Why?

YEAR 1:

YEAR 2:

OCTOBER 31: HAPPY HALLOWEEN!! Will you be trick-or-treating with friends, attending a party, or handing out treats?

YEAR 1:

YEAR 2:

NOVEMBER

NOVEMBER 1: You have to read your winning essay in front of the ENTIRE school! Are you cool as a cucumber or sweating bullets?

YEAR 1:

YEAR 2:

NOVEMBER 2: CONGRATULATIONS! You just opened a new store in the mall! What's the name of your store, and what do you sell?

YEAR 1:

YEAR 2:

NOVEMBER 3: What is your favorite bubble gum flavor?

YEAR 1:

YEAR 2:

NOVEMBER 4: "I'm comfortable being the center of attention when ____________."

YEAR 1:

YEAR 2:

NOVEMBER 5: "It's a little embarrassing to admit, but when no one is looking, I like to ___________."

YEAR 1:

YEAR 2:

NOVEMBER 6: Your crush asks you to hang out at the very same time you're supposed to meet up with your BFFs. What do you do?

YEAR 1:

YEAR 2:

NOVEMBER 7: OMG!! YOU just made the front page of your school newspaper! Details, please! Write the headline below.

YEAR 1:

YEAR 2:

NOVEMBER 8: If you were a dog, what breed would you be and why? Pick out a cute doggy name for yourself.

YEAR 1:

YEAR 2:

NOVEMBER 9: "Although it's tough, I'm trying really hard NOT to ______________."

YEAR 1:

YEAR 2:

NOVEMBER 10: If you could be an exchange student and attend school in another country, what country would it be?

YEAR 1:

YEAR 2:

NOVEMBER 11: Who do you admire most and why?

YEAR 1:

YEAR 2:

NOVEMBER 12: What's your fave color and why?

NIKKI'S ANSWER: Periwinkle, because it's a cute nail polish color and a fun word to say ☺.

YEAR 1:

YEAR 2:

NOVEMBER 13: What was the last test you took in school that was so DIFFICULT it almost made your BRAIN explode? Explain.

YEAR 1:

YEAR 2:

NOVEMBER 14: If you could give away anything that you own to charity, what would it be and why?

YEAR 1:

YEAR 2:

NOVEMBER 15: If you could give away anything that your PARENTS own to charity, what would it be and why?

YEAR 1:

YEAR 2:

NOVEMBER 16: As a sleepover prank, your BFFs wet your clothes and stuff them in the freezer. What do you do?

A) Get mad and go home

B) Laugh it off while drying your clothes

C) Spray whipped cream inside their sleeping bags

OMG!

YEAR 1:

YEAR 2:

NOVEMBER 17: What weird habit does your mom or dad have that drives you crazy?

YEAR 1:

YEAR 2:

NOVEMBER 18: "If I ever get a detention, it will probably be for ____________."

NIKKI'S ANSWER: Hmm . . . probably getting caught writing in my diary during class. But that has NEVER, EVER happened. YET!

YEAR 1:

YEAR 2:

NOVEMBER 19: "I always feel invisible when ________________."

YEAR 1:

YEAR 2:

NOVEMBER 20: Which celeb would make a really cool older sister? Explain.

YEAR 1:

YEAR 2:

NOVEMBER 21: Which celeb would make a really cool older brother? Explain.

YEAR 1:

YEAR 2:

NOVEMBER 22: Whose cooking do you FEAR most? Why?

YEAR 1:

YEAR 2:

NOVEMBER 23: Have you ever pretended to be sick so that you could stay home from school? What did you do, and did it work?

YEAR 1:

YEAR 2:

NOVEMBER 24: Would you rather be the oldest or the youngest child in your family and why?

NIKKI'S ANSWER: I'd like to be the youngest so I could switch places with Brianna and make HER babysit ME! Mwa-hahahaha!!!

YEAR 1:

YEAR 2:

NOVEMBER 25: The shy new girl at school just dropped her book. What do you do?

A) Smile and pick it up for her

B) Introduce yourself and ask her where she's from

C) Invite her to sit with you and your BFFs at lunch

YEAR 1:

YEAR 2:

NOVEMBER 26: "The Thanksgiving food that I LOVE eating is ______________________!"

YEAR 1:

YEAR 2:

NOVEMBER 27: "The Thanksgiving food that is so gross I would secretly feed it to my DOG is ______________________!"

YEAR 1:

YEAR 2:

NOVEMBER 28: The Thanksgiving season is a time for reflection! What are you thankful for?

YEAR 1:

YEAR 2:

NOVEMBER 29: You're invited to attend the very FIRST Thanksgiving dinner back in 1621! What yummy dish will you bring to share?

YEAR 1:

YEAR 2:

NOVEMBER 30: Who would be best at writing a Miss Know-It-All advice column, you or one of your friends? Please explain.

YEAR 1:

YEAR 2:

DECEMBER

DECEMBER 1: You just got six inches of snow! SQUEEEE! Do you build a snowman, go sledding, or make snow angels?

YEAR 1:

YEAR 2:

DECEMBER 2: If you could live inside the world of any BOOK you've read, what book would it be and why?

YEAR 1:

YEAR 2:

DECEMBER 3: If you could live inside the world of any MOVIE you've seen, what movie would it be and why?

YEAR 1:

YEAR 2:

DECEMBER 4: What was the last thing you BEGGED your BFF to do? Explain.

YEAR 1:

YEAR 2:

DECEMBER 5: You and your BFFs decide to take a dance class! Do you choose ballet, tap, jazz, modern, hip-hop, or something else? Explain.

YEAR 1:

YEAR 2:

DECEMBER 6: If you could read anyone's diary without their knowing it, whose would it be and why?

YEAR 1:

YEAR 2:

DECEMBER 7: What GRADES are you trying really hard to earn on your report card this semester? List them below.

YEAR 1:

YEAR 2:

DECEMBER 8: What is the funniest or weirdest DREAM you've had lately? What do you think it meant?

YEAR 1:

YEAR 2:

DECEMBER 9: Are you mostly a TALKER or a LISTENER? Explain.

NIKKI'S ANSWER: I'm probably more of a talker! I'm ALWAYS venting about all the DRAMA in my life ☺.

YEAR 1:

YEAR 2:

DECEMBER 10: Which pampered pooch would you place in your posh purse? A Yorkie, a Chihuahua, or a poodle? Explain.

YEAR 1:

YEAR 2:

DECEMBER 11: If you could switch LIVES with any of your classmates for one week, who would it be and why?

YEAR 1:

YEAR 2:

DECEMBER 12: If you could switch PARENTS with any of your friends for one week, whose would it be and why?

YEAR 1:

YEAR 2:

DECEMBER 13: What kind of cookie could you eat a dozen of in one sitting?

YEAR 1:

YEAR 2:

DECEMBER 14: Are you ticklish? If so, where are your three most ticklish spots?

YEAR 1:

YEAR 2:

DECEMBER 15: Have you ever done something that you've regretted? What was it, and what lesson did you learn?

NIKKI'S ANSWER: I toilet-papered MacKenzie's house as a joke. But I learned that even a harmless prank can sometimes have serious consequences.

YEAR 1:

YEAR 2:

DECEMBER 16: What feels the coziest on a cold winter night: a fleece nightgown, fuzzy pj's, or footie pajamas?

YEAR 1:

YEAR 2:

DECEMBER 17: "I'm always a nervous wreck whenever ____________."

NIKKI'S ANSWER: Whenever we have a test in geometry ☹!

YEAR 1:

YEAR 2:

DECEMBER 18: If you were invisible for a day, where would you go and what would you do?

YEAR 1:

YEAR 2:

DECEMBER 19: Who would you like to meet under the mistletoe?!

YEAR 1:

YEAR 2:

DECEMBER 20: If you could give yourself a brand-new (and very trendy) first and middle name, what would it be?

YEAR 1:

YEAR 2:

DECEMBER 21: When I want to get away from people and CHILLAX, I hide out in the janitor's closet! Where is your secret hideout? Explain.

YEAR 1:

YEAR 2:

DECEMBER 22: Have you been good this year? If so, make a Christmas list to give to Santa! SQUEEE!!

YEAR 1:

YEAR 2:

DECEMBER 23: Many people celebrate a holiday around this time of year. What holiday do YOU and your family celebrate? Details, please.

YEAR 1:

YEAR 2:

DECEMBER 24: Santa needs your help! It's Christmas Eve, and his nine reindeer have the flu! Give him a list of nine reindeer with silly names that can guide his sleigh tonight!

YEAR 1:

YEAR 2:

DECEMBER 25: MERRY CHRISTMAS! Chloe, Zoey, and I wish you a Merry Christmas and a Happy New Year! How has today been really special?

YEAR 1:

YEAR 2:

DECEMBER 26: What gift did you get that you totally didn't expect? What was your favorite gift?

YEAR 1:

YEAR 2:

DECEMBER 27: A brand-new year is right around the corner! What's your BEST memory of THIS year? Explain.

YEAR 1:

YEAR 2:

DECEMBER 28: You just stumbled upon some magic seeds! Once planted, a TREE will grow that produces an endless supply of any one thing you request. What grows on YOUR tree?

YEAR 1:

YEAR 2:

DECEMBER 29: YOU'RE making a diary just like MINE! SQUEEE! List five exciting things you plan to write about that would have me DYING to read it!

YEAR 1:

YEAR 2:

DECEMBER 30: Now think up a cool title for your diary and write it below!

YEAR 1:

YEAR 2:

DECEMBER 31: It's New Year's Eve! What are your plans to celebrate the new year?

YEAR 1:

YEAR 2:

OMG!! IT'S THE END OF THE YEAR!!

But we have SO much more to talk about! Go back to the beginning of your diary to start an exciting new year. By the time you've filled up the entire book, you'll have two years of awesome entries you'll want to read over and over again.

You can keep your *OMG! All About Me Diary!* all to yourself or share it with your BFFs. Who knows?! Maybe one day your diary will become a really popular book series! How cool would that be?! ☺!

I really enjoyed YOUR answers to all of MY questions! Now, what question have YOU been dying to ask ME?!

Rachel Renée Russell is an attorney who prefers writing tween books to legal briefs. (Mainly because books are a lot more fun and pajamas and bunny slippers aren't allowed in court.)

She has raised two daughters and lived to tell about it. Her hobbies include growing purple flowers and doing totally useless crafts (like, for example, making a microwave oven out of Popsicle sticks, glue, and glitter). Rachel lives in northern Virginia with a spoiled pet Yorkie who terrorizes her daily by climbing on top of a computer cabinet and pelting her with stuffed animals while she writes. And, yes, Rachel considers herself a total Dork.